presents:

Mini-Putt & Bike Ride

Story 1

Mini-Putt

Written by: Sam Goolamallee

Illustrated by: Jonathan Coit

Dedicated to the trio,
I couldn't have done this
without you.

Library and Archives Canada Cataloguing Publication
Goolamallee, Sam,
HighField World Mini-Putt & Bike Ride / Sam Goolamallee ;
Illustrated by Jonathan Coit
ISBN: 978-0-9919402-2-6

HighField World: Mini Putt & Bike Ride
Published by OCC Inc.
Ottawa, ON, Canada

Written by: Sam Goolamallee
Illustrated by: Jonathan Coit
Edited by: Allison Gibson
Layout and design: Martin Murtonen

Visit us at www.highfieldworld.com

Printed in USA

During breakfast, Dad wondered what he and the kids would do on such a nice day.

WHAT TO DO? WHAT TO DO? WHAT TO DO ON A *NICE DAY* LIKE TODAY?

HOW ABOUT A GAME OF *MINI-PUTT*?

Mini-putt sounded like a great idea!

And Dad said...

IF WE WORK TOGETHER, WE'LL BE READY FASTER.

GO TO THE BATHROOM, BRUSH YOUR TEETH, AND GET ALL "THAT BUSINESS" DONE...

SUNSCREEN. AND WE'RE OFF TO MINI-PUTT!

LET'S GET SOME THINGS DONE BEFORE WE GO.

Of course, once they got to mini-putt, Dad explained some of the basic rules so there'd be no craziness!

NOW BEFORE WE PLAY, LET'S MAKE SURE WE UNDERSTAND THE RULES OF MINI-PUTT.

1. KEEP THE MINI-PUTT STICK DOWN LOW. THE MINI-PUTT STICK IS CALLED A "PUTTER".

DON'T LET THE PUTTER GO ABOVE YOUR SHORTS WHEN YOU SWING IT.

2. NO RUNNING OR YELLING BECAUSE IT DISTRACTS THE OTHER PLAYERS.

3. LISTEN TO WHAT DADDY IS SAYING BECAUSE DADDY RULES!

4. HAVE FUN!

5

Dad, explained...

THERE ARE **LOTS** OF **NUMBERS** ON THE MINI-PUTT COURSE.

WE **FOLLOW** THE NUMBERS LIKE A PUZZLE STARTING AT 1 AND GOING TO 18.

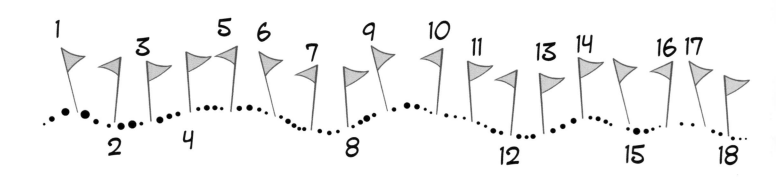

GOOD THING WE CAN ALL COUNT TO 18!

OK, AZON, FREDDY, PICK A BALL!

7

Because Dad had spent years becoming a mini-putt super-master, he took the time to show the kids the way to hit a ball with the putter.

THIS IS HOW I STAND TO HIT THE BALL WITH THE PUTTER.

Dad carefully placed his feet.

I MAKE A PRETEND TRIANGLE, WITH MY FEET AS THE BOTTOM OF THE TRIANGLE, AND THE BALL IS THE TOP OF THE TRIANGLE.

He then swung the putter and said,

WHEN YOU SWING, MAKE SURE YOU KEEP YOUR EYES ON THE BALL.

Dad coached Azon on how to stand, swing the putter, and hit the ball.

Dad continued to explain how the game is played.

Freddy's turn. She had a bit of a hard time putting the ball, but then she remembered how Dad did it. Still, it took practice.

I'M GOING TO HIT MY BALL TO THE HOLE.

WHOOPS! I NEED TO HOLD THE PUTTER WITH *TWO HANDS* SO I CAN MAKE THE BALL GO WHERE I WANT.

Azon was on a roll, and got totally excited.

DADDY! DAD!, HEY, DAD! LOOK AT *ME* HIT THE BALL.

AZON, I CAN SEE YOU NO PROBLEM LITTLE MAN, BUT YOU NEED TO REMEMBER THE RULES. NO YELLING AND NO SWINGING THE PUTTER ABOVE YOUR SHORTS.

NOW LET'S GET BACK AND *HAVE FUN* PLAYING THE GAME.

Azon's ball got stuck on the mini-putt course.

MY BALL'S STUCK. I CAN PICK UP THE BALL AND PUT IT IN THE MIDDLE SO I CAN HIT IT.

Dad then noticed Azon doing something silly.

LITTLE MAN! YOU'RE
BEING SILLY. YOU CAN
WALK AROUND THE
BRIDGE!

Then Dad noticed Freddy...

It seems Dad forgot rule number 4.

Azon completed the 9th hole and waited for Freddy. Well done, Azon!

Freddy also got her ball into the hole. Well done, Freddy!

As they played, Dad explained how to be courteous playing mini-putt.

WHEN SOMEONE HAS FINISHED A HOLE, IT'S POLITE TO WAIT FOR THE REST OF THE GROUP TO FINISH, THEN PICK UP YOUR BALL BEFORE GOING TO THE NEXT NUMBER.

On the 18th hole of the mini-putt course, Azon tapped his ball straight into the hole...and the ball disappeared! It took a few tries, but Freddy also tapped her ball into the hole.

They tried to see where their balls went but they were gone. Where did they go? Dad explained,

THAT'S HOW THEY COLLECT THE BALLS AT THE END OF THE GAME.

THEY GO INTO A COLLECTOR BUCKET BEHIND THE WALL.

THAT GAME WAS FUN. TIME TO HEAD FOR HOME.

On the way to the car, Dad reminded Freddy and Azon...

Once in the car, Dad congratulated Freddy and Azon for a good game.

EVERYONE DID AN AWESOME JOB AT FOLLOWING THE RULES AND PLAYING MINI-PUTT.

21

Once everyone was inside, Dad said,

AZON, PLACE
YOUR SHOES NICELY
AND WASH YOUR
HANDS PLEASE. YOU
TOO, FREDDY!

Azon and Freddy then said happily,

THANKS
FOR TAKING US
TO MINI-PUTT,
DAD!

THE END

presents:

Mini-Putt & Bike Ride

Story 2

Bike Ride

Written by: Sam Goolamallee

Illustrated by: Jonathan Coit

Dedicated to: Azan,
Being a first born is pretty hard...
...its also pretty special.
I'm very proud of you.

Library and Archives Canada Cataloguing
Publication
Goolamallee, Sam,
Highfield World Mini-Putt & Bike Ride / Sam
Goolamallee ; Illustrated by Jonathan Coit
ISBN 978-0-9919402-2-6

Highfield World: Highfield World: Mini Putt & Bike
RidePublished by OCC Inc.
Ottawa, ON, Canada
Copyright © 2014 Sam Goolamallee and OCC Inc.

Written by: Sam Goolamallee
Illustrated by: Jonathan Coit
Edited by: Allison Gibson
Layout and design: Martin Murtonen

Visit us at www.highfieldworld.com

It was a beautiful day, and Dad came up with a great idea.

Azon was excited to go, but before they left, they had to prepare.

WE HAVE TO GET READY BEFORE WE GO ON OUR RIDE.

LET'S START IN THE KITCHEN TO FIND WHAT WE NEED.

In the kitchen, Dad asked Azon for some help.

Azon happily loaded up the back-pack.

29

Once the back-pack was full, Dad and Azon were almost ready! They still had to...

...put on some sunscreen...

...their shoes...

...and helmets.

Their gear was on, but they needed to go over just a few more things. Like lefts and rights.

AZON, HOW ARE YOU WITH YOUR LEFTS AND RIGHTS?

I'M OK DAD.

I'M GOING TO SHOW YOU A LITTLE SOMETHING TO DO **BEFORE** YOU GET ON YOUR BIKE...

REMEMBER, THAT'S FOR PRACTICE BEFORE YOU GET ON YOUR BIKE.

...**BEFORE!** NOT WHILE YOU'RE ON YOUR BIKE.

IF YOU HOLD UP YOUR HANDS LIKE THIS, THE ONE THAT MAKES THE "L" IS YOUR LEFT HAND.

WHEN YOU'RE ON YOUR BIKE, YOUR HANDS ARE ON THE HANDLES AT ALL TIMES, LITTLE MAN.

31

They also reviewed some safety rules.

LET'S GO OVER SOME SAFETY RULES
BEFORE WE GET ON OUR BIKES:

1) KEEP YOUR HANDS ON THE BIKE HANDLES.

2) STAY ON THE RIGHT SIDE OF THE BIKE PATH.

3) LISTEN TO WHAT DADDY SAYS AT ALL TIMES.

As they rode down the path, Azon went over one of the rules in his head.

I HAVE TO REMEMBER TO STAY ON THE RIGHT-HAND SIDE OF THE BIKE PATH AND FOLLOW DAD.

I STAY ON THE RIGHT SIDE OF THE BIKE-PATH SO THAT I DON'T CRASH INTO BIKES COMING THE OTHER WAY.

After riding their bikes for a while, Azon and Dad found a good place to stop for a drink.

When they finished their water break, they jumped back on their bikes and Azon took the lead!

It's a good thing Azon listened to Dad! If he didn't look ahead he might have run into a mama goose and her babies crossing the bike path.

OH! WE'RE STOPPING BECAUSE A GOOSE AND HER GOSLINGS ARE CROSSING THE BIKE PATH. THIS MUST BE A GOOSE CROSSING!

YOU KNOW THE WORD *"GOSLINGS"* AZON? I'M IMPRESSED!

While they waited for the mama goose and her goslings to cross the path, Azon asked about the bell on his bike.

Azon jumped on his bike to test the bell out.
He was so excited, he let out a cheer.

Dad and Azon rode for a little while longer. They stopped at the beach to snack on some mangos and watch people play volleyball.

THE BEACH IS A GOOD PLACE TO STOP AND HAVE OUR SNACKS. WE CAN WATCH PEOPLE PLAYING VOLLEYBALL ON THE SAND.

I LOVE MANGOS!

After their snack, Dad and Azon kept going down the bike path along the river. Going up the hills was hard. Going down the hills was easy.

Dad reminded Azon to be ready to use his brakes when going downhill.

Azon and Dad took one more break near some rocks down by the river. Careful with the wobbly rocks, Azon!

On the last part of the ride, Dad and Azon were both tired, so they pedaled just a little slower on their way home.

Join the Highfeld World Kids in their next adventure at the Street Party!

Find more information about **HIGHFIELD WORLD**
at *www.highfieldworld.com*

Made in the USA
Charleston, SC
12 February 2017